FOLKTALES AND LEGENDS OF WARWICKSHIRE

Merlin Price

CONTENTS

ONE-HANDED BOUGHTON

The Boughton family lived at Lawford Hall at Little Lawford near Rugby. The ghost of One-Handed Boughton continued to haunt the area up until the end of the Second World War.

The electricity that drained to earth near Lawford Hall claimed a rare victim on that sweltering hot evening midway through the reign of Elizabeth I. The storm had been brewing for days and when the lightning struck across the fields it heralded one of Warwickshire's strangest stories: the tale of One-Handed Boughton.

His Lordship was making his way back towards the Hall from across the fields when the storm released its pent-up thunderbolt. With a tremendous explosion a jagged sheet of forked lightning crashed towards the unfortunate Earl and pinned him to the ground. Servants ran screaming across the meadow and hurriedly made the sign of the cross at the sight of their dead master. Imagine their shock and surprise when, drawing near to the corpse, his Lordship sat up and appeared to be none the worse for his ordeal. It was only then, amidst the expressions of surprise and relief that the coachman, with a horrified gasp, pointed towards his Lordship's sleeve. His right hand was gone. All that remained was a charred stump of flesh and the singed ends of the sleeve. He was carried back to the Hall and showed every sign of having made a remarkable recovery. However, from that day onwards his mood darkened.

Many of those employed on the estate muttered about the unnatural manner by which he had cheated the Angel of Death. It was not right and proper, they said, that a man struck by God's hand should survive unharmed. Many began to whisper of a pact with the Devil. From that day he was called 'One-Handed Boughton' and the name took on more than a hint of menace.

In the fullness of time Lord Boughton's life ran to its natural end, and after the funeral service life returned to normal at the Hall.

Normal that is except for one detail. Not one person could spend the night in the bedchamber previously occupied by the late Lord. Each person who tried complained of a heavy and oppressive atmosphere, such as gathers before a storm, followed by apparitions and noises as befitted the Devil and his works. It was also at this time that reports were heard of One-Handed Boughton riding across the neighbouring lands in a coach and six. The haunting of the bed chamber increased in malevolence, with hapless visitors being driven from the room terrified and with their wits turned.

Such was the intensity of the phenomena, and the mounting number of reports of the phantom coach and six terrorising the neighbourhood, that Sir Edward Boughton, in the Year of Our Lord 1752, decided to lay the ghost once and for all. He called upon a team of twelve clergymen, led by the renowned Parson Hall of Great Harborough. Upon that evening they gathered at the foot of the great staircase of the Hall and solemnly lit the twelve candles of exorcism.

Armed with bell, book and candles, they made their way towards the bedchamber of One-Handed Boughton. Parson Hall halted at the doorway, feeling the unnatural chill of the room. He reached within his vestments and took out a green glass phial and stopper. The silence was broken by the sound of a thin dank wind springing up from the far side of the room, even though the casements and windows were shut tight. As the twelve clergymen made their way into the chamber the wind increased and began to pluck at their clothing. Some of the candles flickered and were snuffed out. All the noisome vapours of the Pit were then released into the confined space of the bedroom and several of the priests gagged and vomited in their horror. Soon eleven of the twelve candles were extinguished and an evil presence was felt by all who stood in the room. Parson Hall fought valiantly against the Powers of Darkness, and shouting out the commands of exorcism, he held the glass phial aloft.
'Audi ergo, et time Santana, inimice fidei, hostis generis humsni....'
The wind howled about the room. The more fainthearted of the priests cowered in a corner as Parson Hall continued the liturgy.
'Recede ergo in nomine Patris et filii et spiritus sancti.....'

With that the room grew calm and the final candle began to flicker. The old priest's eyes widened. Should this last candle be extinguished then the battle would be lost and their souls would be forfeit.

'Recede!' he cried again, 'I conjure you into this phial!' He paused, trying to reclaim his waning strength. 'I conjure you but declare that you may be released a little season to wander abroad!'

Upon this bargain being spoken there was a monstrous sigh, and Parson Hall quickly seized the stopper and sealed the phial. The room returned to normal. The eleven other priests offered up a prayer of thanksgiving and with rather unseemly haste the phial was taken to an old marl pit in the grounds of the Hall and consigned to the muddy depths.

Despite this exorcism the hauntings continued, and then, in 1780, Sir Theodosius, now the head of the Boughton family, was murdered by his brother-in-law, a Captain Donellan. Donellan paid the ultimate penalty on the gallows at Warwick the following year. By now Boughton Hall was clearly tainted with evil, and four years later orders were given by the remaining family for it to be demolished. There was a great reluctance on the part of the local workmen to take part in this endeavour as they knew only too well the supernatural tales associated with the Hall. However, eventually it was destroyed and the ghost of One-Handed Boughton slumbered a while.

Then, in the nineteenth century a strange bottle was recovered from a pond near the site of the Hall and almost immediately reports were heard again of a ghostly coach and six making its rounds of the neighbourhood. The glass phial was exhibited in Rugby, and many folk came to wonder at the thought of the unseen occupant.

After several months it was taken by the Boughton family and locked in a great wooden casket.

Throughout the Second World War strange stories circulated about the haunting of Brownsover Hall, a nearby estate to Lawford, where the descendants of One-Handed Boughton now lived.

To try to put a stop to the hauntings the bottle was buried in a private ceremony. First though, it was set in a solid protective blanket of cement. Since then the ghost of One-Handed Boughton has not been seen driving his demonic carriage through the dark lanes, and calling to late-night travellers to stand aside. But one can only wonder, just how safe is that bottle's final resting place?

THE TOAD PLOUGH

In times gone by local folk felt free to wander the fields and woodlands of Warwickshire; in more recent times some newcomers have felt the need to limit the access to their land. But they interfere with the Old Ways at their peril.

'What the devil do you think you're doing on my land?'

The old man straightened wearily and pulling his tattered coat tighter around his frail body he glanced in the direction of the voice.

'I said what the devil are you doing trespassing on my land? This land is private! Understand? Private! I don't want any old Tom, Dick or Harry trampling all over the place. What are you doing here anyway?' The irate landowner glared at the old man.

'Always come here. They like what I find here. Slugs, things like that. Taste different from round here.'

'What the hell are you talking about?' exploded the landowner. 'Clear off! And remember from now on this land is private!'

The old man lifted his head slowly and met the landowner's gaze. Then carefully turning his head he spat on the ground and shuffled back onto the footpath towards the road.

The bar of the local inn was crowded. The landlord swiftly filled a pewter tankard and handed it to its owner.

'Old Arthur's down in the dumps right enough tonight!'

He indicated with a nod to where the old man sat staring moodily into his pint of beer.

'What's up with him?'

'That new bloke. The one who bought Glebe Farm. Seems he has a dislike of folk walking across his fields. Tore a strip off Arthur this morning. Hasn't half upset him. He's sat there all night and not said a word to anyone.'

The customer took a deep draught of his beer.

'That new owner will need to watch his step. I wouldn't like to cross Arthur. I've heard too many stories over the years. He's not one to get on the wrong side of.'

The landlord listened intently. He'd only recently taken over the pub and was keen to learn more about his regulars.

'How do you mean?'

The customer drained his tankard and handed it back to the landlord.

'Oh, nothing really,' he paused, 'It's just, well, a few years ago someone upset Arthur and it seemed they fell into a run of bad luck. Just coincidence I suppose. But folk did talk at the time. Drove the farmer out of business in the end so they reckoned. Mind, it was a long time ago.'

The door of the pub was flung open to admit the new owner of Glebe Farm. He stepped up to the bar and smiled amiably at the regulars.

'Gin and tonic, and one for yourself landlord!'

The landlord filled a glass and added a slice of lemon and some ice-cubes.

'Settling in OK then sir?' the customer next to him inquired before drinking deeply from his fresh tankard of beer.

The newcomer grunted.

'Too many damned people taking advantage of me, that's the trouble. Think they can walk over my land as if it belonged to them. Only this morning I had to see someone off my top field. Well I tell you, the next time I find anyone trespassing, it'll be court for 'em and no mistake!'

The landowner sipped delicately at his gin and tonic and the customer drained his tankard and placed it back on the bar.

'I'd best be on my way. Now you look after that land of yours sir, but a word of advice. Try not to go upsettin' old Arthur again.' He nodded in the direction of the old man.

'And what the hell do you mean by that?' spluttered the landowner.

'Nothing sir, nothing at all. Just like I says, try not to upset him. You don't want any trouble from his toads now do you? Well I'll bid you good night. Good night Bernard!'

And with that he headed for the door.

'Toads?' the landowner stared incredulously at the old man huddled in the corner.

'Toads?'

The landlord shrugged his shoulders. He was just as much in the dark himself. The landowner finished his drink.

'Well, must be off!'

'Right you are sir, now mind how you go.'

A few minutes later old Arthur also rose to his feet and shuffled out of the door without a goodnight to any of the assembled regulars.

The old man carefully unlocked the back door of his cottage. Without switching on the light he stepped into the kitchen and began to croon in a strange guttural voice. A rasping noise came from the kitchen floor followed by a sharp movement.

The old man knelt down, still crooning gently. He carefully picked up the toad and stroked its warty skin and flexed its webbed toes. There was further movement across the floor and soon his arms were full of toads, their skins glistening in the moonlight. He opened a cupboard next to the sink and took out a cardboard box. He deftly slid the toads into it and made his way out into the street.

Soon he found himself on the road opposite the top field of Glebe Farm. With a nimbleness that belied his age he hopped over the fence and made his way to the far end of the field. There he carefully removed the lid from the cardboard box and withdrew a small structure of wooden staves and fine leather thongs. One by one he placed his toads in front of this miniature plough and with great care fastened a toad to each of the tiny harnesses. His eyes gleamed as he placed the plough and its bizarre beasts of burden onto the first furrow of the field. The tiny plough trundled its way across the furrow, the toads sweating out an evil-smelling milky liquid onto the fertile ground. When the creatures had ploughed their own small furrow the old man swept them back into their box and vanished into the night.

By early summer the fields of Glebe Farm were still barren.

'Just no crops at all. I've had the people round from the Ministry but they haven't a clue. They say there's no disease.'

The newcomer was holding forth to his cronies in the bar of the village pub. 'To crown it all I found that damned old man trespassing on my fields again last week. Gave me a ridiculous story about how one of his toads was sick and needing a certain type of beetle to cure it. I told him to push off and find his precious beetles elsewhere. He gave me a load of abuse so I've decided to teach him a lesson. I've been to the police station and preferred charges against him for trespass. That should stop him and his beetle-drives!' He laughed heartily at his joke.

One of the regulars drained his pint and shook his head sorrowfully as he got up to leave. As he reached the door he half muttered to himself.
'I did warn you. I knew you'd have trouble with those toads if you didn't watch out.'
'Eh?' the new landowner turned. 'Did you mention toads again?'
But the man had gone.

The old man closed the kitchen door as the village policeman climbed onto his bicycle and pedalled away. With shaking fingers he placed the summons on the draining board. He paused for a moment and then began to call his pets in the same crooning tone. They quickly appeared and began to climb onto his hands. One, more feeble than the rest, hopped ineffectually at his leg. The old man picked it up and stroked it lovingly. Tears began to form in his eyes. He gently placed the ailing toad on the floor and began to rummage at the back of an old pine cupboard that stood inside the pantry. After a while he emerged clutching an even more battered cardboard box covered in the dust of many years. He wiped it with his sleeve and began to gather up his toads and place them inside. Closing the back door behind him he made his way in the darkness towards Glebe Farm.

The new landowner weaved his way somewhat unsteadily into the car park of the village pub and slumped into the driver's seat of his new Jaguar. He swerved into the road and within minutes was sweeping up the drive to his farm. He failed to notice the bent figure hugging the hedgerows as the car whispered by. He parked the car in the garage and made his way into the house. His wife had long since gone to bed. He stepped into the drawing room and poured himself a nightcap. He sank gratefully into his armchair and as he sipped his drink he began to recall the details of his row with the impudent trespasser.

The doorbell rang.

Frowning slightly he made his way into the hall.

The bell rang again.

'All right, I'm coming! I'm coming!'

He flung open the door.

As the fatal heart attack devoured his chest, his last sight was of a team of glistening toads, their twisted limbs harnessed by fine leather thongs to an intricately fashioned miniature of an eighteenth-century hearse.

ILMINGTON RIVALRY

Rivalry between neighbouring villages is not exactly unknown in Warwickshire. Such a rivalry existed between the village of Ilmington and its neighbour Ebrington, just over the border in Gloucestershire. Many tales were spread by the people of Ilmington about the somewhat limited mental powers of Ebrington folk.

'Taller!'

There was a murmur of agreement around the table and ale was quaffed to confirm that opinion.

'By rights our church tower should be the tallest around. That'd give them folk from Ilmington less cause for talk!'

There was further muttered agreement and calls for liquid refreshment.

The parson gazed around the company of village elders.

'Only one trouble,' he said, 'we have no money for such an undertaking as building a new tower.'

There was a silence, broken only by the continued muttering of 'Taller!' from Benjamin Morris, whose hearing was not of the best.

The parson glared him into silence.

Tommy Harris raised his mug and drank deeply. Wiping his hand against his mouth, he spoke. 'No money for building a new tower? What I say is what's the matter with the old one?'

'Taller! It needs to be taller!' burbled the venerable Benjamin. This time the entire company froze him to silence.

'Aye, well perhaps he's not that wrong,' continued Tommy Harris. 'Tell us, what do we do to make it grow?'

'Grow? Grow? Whoever heard of a church tower that could grow?' responded the parson.

'With respect, each to his own trade,' replied Master Harris, 'we're all farmers and if there's one thing we know is what gets things to grow!'

There was noisy agreement around the table and further strengthening draughts were supped.

'Muck!' called out Benjamin Morris, entering into the spirit of the discussion. 'Good honest muck! That's what's needed! Never fails!'

The row of bucolic heads nodded like the corn they nourished in their fields and the parson raised his eyes to heaven as the stalwart farmers agreed to meet at the church tower the following afternoon.

The next day threatened rain, but the six farmers arrived and soon set to work unloading their carts of good strong manure. With pitchforks they stacked the aromatic cure against the walls of the tower. Soon a layer three feet high had been plastered around the stonework.

The men stood back to admire their work.

'Now that should do the trick,' announced Tommy Harris. 'My manure has been rotting down for seven years, and everything it touches does grow twice as high I do swear!'

The others joined in with confirmation of the potency of their particular noisome mix.

'Quick! Before we go we need to measure!' cried old Benjamin, and hurrying up to the tower he carefully placed his wooden staff against the ground and marked off the height to the top of the flavoursome pile. The rain began to pour down and so the satisfied farmers repaired to the local inn. After several jugs of strong ale Tommy Harris drew attention to the fact that the rain had stopped. Around the church tower the rain had neatly compressed the pile. Benjamin Morris and his measuring staff were first on the scene. He turned to the others and crowed, 'A good six inches already!' The farmers returned home in good cheer.

Six weeks later those same worthies were again sat around their table in the local inn. Again it was Benjamin Morris who spoke.

'It needs to be taller!'

Again there was muttered agreement, added to this time by a number of disheartened comments as to why the initial spurt of growth had not been sustained.

The parson spoke up.

'Now it is my turn to suggest a remedy. As obviously the tower is incapable of further growth, the simple answer is to make it appear taller!'

'Now how on earth do we do that?' queried Tommy Harris, still smarting from the defeat of his powerful manure.

'Simple,' replied the good reverend. 'We push the tower further up the hill!'

There was another silence. Several mouthfuls of ale were required to help swallow the parson's solution, but nevertheless, on the following afternoon the six sturdy farmers and the parson were to be found examining the footings of the tower and the slope of the adjoining hillside.

The parson pointed to the wall opposite the hill.

'We shall push from there,' he decreed.

Benjamin Morris scratched his head. 'We need to know when to stop,' he reasoned. 'We don't want to push it too far.'

'Good thinking!' cried the vicar. 'Strip off your coats and we'll lay them down on the other side of the tower. That will give us a measure.'

The six farmers dutifully laid down their coats and trooped to the opposite wall of the tower.

'Heave!' The parson and his men bent to their task.

'Heave!'

For half an hour they toiled and strained, and such was their concentration that they neither saw nor heard two tinkers approach the tower and exclaim at their good fortune in finding seven fine coats. Not wishing to over-extend their good fortune, the tinkers then beat a hasty retreat.

'One last heave!'

The farmers obliged and then released their hold.

'I swear by our efforts we've pushed it half a mile,' gasped Tommy Harris.

'Let's find out for ourselves,' declared the vicar.

They made their way around the tower to collect their coats and stopped, amazed.

'The Good Lord bless us!' cried Benjamin.

The others stared at him.

'We've pushed the tower so far we've gone and pushed it over our coats!'

A look of great pride at their achievement spread over the faces of the six farmers and the parson as they made their way down to the inn to celebrate. And one by one they turned as they walked away to comment on how much taller the church tower looked, now that it was indeed further up the hill.

THE PHANTOM LORRY

Drivers on the A45 Coventry to Rugby road have often been terrified by a lorry careering towards them on the wrong side of the road.

It was a cold winter's night in the nineteen fifties. The unkind providence that had blanketed the whole of the Midlands in fog that day had now redoubled its efforts and was supplying a steady downfall of snow.

Driving conditions on the narrow stretch of the A45 near Knightlow changed from being merely unpleasant to downright treacherous within a few minutes. Visibility was down to a few yards as the local constable lifted the curtain in his living room and tut-tutted at the speed with which traffic was still travelling down the main road. He had barely replaced the curtains when the scream of brakes and the squeal of rubber being flayed from protesting tyres brought him rushing to the door. He felt rather than heard the impact in the thick fog beyond his house. A large lorry had skidded, and, desperately trying to right itself, had turned over onto its side.

Within seconds, as the policeman was hurrying towards the scene, a car's headlights pierced the fog. It was travelling far too quickly to respond to the danger ahead. Helplessly the constable watched as the driver jammed on his brakes, but to no avail. The car slammed into the overturned lorry and slewed around. The two vehicles were now completely blocking the road.

As the policeman hurried towards the wreckage the terrible realisation dawned on him that he had no way of warning other traffic that might be approaching through the fog. Sure enough, before his horrified gaze further vehicles hurtled out of the darkness and crashed into the wreckage ahead.

He racked his brains for some means of preventing further terrible accidents. He had succeeded in the meantime in pulling many of the drivers from their vehicles, and now an idea came to him.

16

Quickly gathering together a handful of uninjured men, he instructed them to pull down as many branches as they could from the surrounding hedgerows and drag them back up the road. In a few minutes a great pile was erected in the middle of the road some hundred yards back from the crash site. The bonfire was quickly set alight, acting as a warning beacon to approaching vehicles and allowing them time to slow down before they reached the scene of the pile-up.

The policeman's main concern was now with the injured. He was just about to turn back towards the crashed vehicles to check that everyone had got out, when a voice called out, 'Here comes another one!'

Twin cones of light cut through the fog, and in an instant a great lorry, its load covered by a black tarpaulin, hurtled out of the darkness. The policeman was aghast. How could the driver not have seen the warning fire up ahead? As the lorry sped past he turned and began to run after it. It was then that he noticed that the flames of the fire appeared to be shining brightly through the juggernaut. He braced himself for the inevitable impact as the lorry plunged towards the wreckage.

But there was no crash.

No scream of tortured metal or the crack of splintering glass.

And no lorry.

THE SAINT VALENTINE'S DAY MURDER

This grim murder story at the end of the Second World War involved dark forces. Even all the skills of Fabian, Scotland Yard's most famous detective, failed to bring the killer to book. Witchcraft, which has always been prevalent in Warwickshire, was not ruled out.

Saint Valentine's Day 1945 heralded the beginnings of an early spring after a freezing Cotswold winter. Seventy-four year old Charles Walton, a man who had lived in Lower Quinton all his life, surveyed the change in the weather and decided that it would be a fine day for some hedging. He set off from his cottage soon after nine o'clock that morning carrying with him a long-handled slash-hook and a hay fork. He had decided to work in a field up on the slopes of Meon Hill.

Charles Walton was something of an enigma. He was said to converse with birds and other small animals, and some people regarded him as a bit of a crank. Others saw him as a quiet, inoffensive man who kept himself to himself. He had worked on the land all his life and had always kept strict time in the work he was hired to do. It was always his way to be back home by four o'clock come rain or shine. So when his niece called at his cottage at six o'clock that evening and found he had not returned, she immediately felt that something was wrong. It was dark by then and Charles Walton was not one to stay out after nightfall. His niece called on the farmer whose fields he had been hedging and they both leapt to the conclusion that he may have been taken ill. Together with his neighbour the farmer made his way towards the field where Walton had last been seen working. The two men reached the field and saw before them a dreadful and macabre sight. The old man lay close to an old willow tree and his face was contorted into a hideous grimace of terror. He lay impaled through the neck with his own pitchfork, the tines bent and thrust six inches into the ground. His slash-hook blade lay embedded deep in his chest. His face, or rather what was left of it, had been slashed and across his throat and chest were two deeper slashes which formed the shape of a cross.

The police were lost for a motive. Old Charles Walton had lived a simple life and appeared to have no enemies. The only item missing from his body was an old tin watch. However, considering the village contained only around five hundred souls, the police felt that the murderer would not be too hard to find. Their first theory was that the crime had been committed by a mad man. It was not long before Scotland Yard was called in to help solve the mystery. Detective Superintendent Fabian, the renowned detective, arrived at Lower Quinton to take over the inquiry. By now the police had begun to suspect that the murder was the work of one of the foreign prisoners of war held at the POW camp at Long Marston. Every single prisoner at the camp was questioned, some at great length. The interrogations revealed one clue. An Italian had been seen scrubbing blood off his clothes, and a witness said they had seen him crouched in a ditch not far from the scene of the murder wiping blood from his hands. His clothing was swiftly dispatched to the forensic lab and the police began to consider the case solved. The report that came back from the lab stated 'rabbit blood'. The prisoner had been indulging in nothing more serious than some illicit poaching. At the inquest the jury returned a verdict of 'murder by person or persons unknown'.

Meanwhile Superintendent Fabian continued his search for fresh clues and paced the slopes of Meon Hill time and time again. One evening on the hillside just before dark a big black dog ran past him. A few moments later a young farm lad appeared along the path. Fabian inquired as to whether he was looking for his dog.
'What dog?' asked the boy.
'A large black dog,' replied Fabian.
The boy paused for a moment and then, with a look of sheer panic on his face, he ran as fast as he could until he was out of sight of the detective. That night at the local inn Fabian mentioned the incident. The locals' eyes widened as they listened to the details, and they pointed out that for many a years a ghost dog had haunted the hillside. The story was that some forty years before, a young farm hand had seen the dog on his way home. For nine consecutive nights the lad had seen it, and on the ninth night the dog changed into a headless woman dressed in black, who glided silently past the boy.

The following day the boy's sister died unexpectedly. The farm lad's name was Charles Walton.

As Fabian began to make further inquiries he became aware of a hostile wall of silence surrounding the village. People became less eager to talk, and at the local inn the conversation became more subdued whenever the detective entered the bar. All that the police were able to pick up were guarded comments and whispered gossip that this murder had involved something even more sinister than a violent lunatic. It was then that Fabian discovered the startling resemblance to another crime that led back through the years to the practice of witchcraft.

In 1875 in the nearby village of Long Compton, Ann Tennant, an old woman of more than eighty years, was murdered. She had been found impaled through the neck and eye by a pitchfork. A farm labourer named John Haywood was arrested, the bloodied pitchfork still in his hands. At his trial at Warwick Assizes he declared that Ann Tennant had been a witch and that he had been cursed by her. He also claimed that there were sixteen other witches in the village and that they all deserved to be put to death in a like manner. He called upon the judge to weigh the old woman's body against the Church Bible, an ancient means of determining a witch. He also called for a glass phial to be brought into court and to be filled with his own urine. When the phial was inverted bubbles formed in it, a sure sign, he cried, of his possession by witchcraft. 'It were the only way to be rid of her,' he averred. 'Her had to be pinned to the ground and marked with the sign of the cross. There be no other way to ruinate a witch!'

Pinned to the ground and marked with the sign of the cross – and Charles Walton had perished in exactly the same manner!

Superintendent Fabian had only a short time to assimilate this incredible connection before two other incidents involving the black dog took place.

A young boy walking along the edge of Meon Hill, near the spot where Charles Walton's body had been discovered, saw a strange form hanging from a nearby tree. On closer examination it proved to be the body of a large black dog, hung high in the branches and strangled by its own collar. How it came to be there was never discovered. A week later a police car ran over and killed another black dog in the lanes near Meon Hill. The next day a calf died suddenly at a nearby farm for no apparent reason, and despite the early spring, the crops in the area were sickly and sparse. Those few village folk who could be persuaded to talk began to mutter about witchcraft.

As the weeks turned to months no further progress was made in the hunt for Walton's killer and eventually Superintendent Fabian returned to London, but the case was not forgotten. Superintendent Spooner, the local police officer in charge of the case, returned to the village each Saint Valentine's Day, stationing himself beneath the willow tree where Walton's body had been found. He hoped perhaps that the murderer might return to the scene of the crime. But no one ever appeared.

The murder gradually became absorbed into the folklore of the village and over the years the memory of the dreadful crime faded. That is until one day in the summer of 1960. A builder discovered an old watch in what had been Charles Walton's back garden. A great deal of re-building was taking place and the watch had been discovered beneath what had once been a garden shed. It was shown to some of Charles Walton's acquaintances and one of them seized the watch and carefully prised open the back. He shook his head. 'That ain't his watch,' he pronounced.
The police wanted to know how he could be so sure.
'It ain't got his shrivening glass in it,' was the reply.
After further questioning it was revealed that Walton had always carried concealed in his watchcase a jet black glass. Not a spectacle lens or an ordinary magnifying glass, but a strange polished object that was like glass but in some mysterious way different. The police recalled that the only item removed from the body had been an old tin watch, virtually valueless, and no real motive for robbery.

So, was the glass in truth a 'shrivening glass', a witch's mirror used as a means of foreseeing the future? Was this at long last the evidence of Charles Walton's connection with the 'Old Ways', and was it this item his killer sought, rather than the watch itself? Had the old man been involved in Black Magic, placing a curse on crops and animals in the village? At Scotland Yard the file on Charles Walton's murder remains open.

The Saint Valentine's Day Murder remains unsolved.

A POACHER CHANGES PROFESSION

Charlecote Deer Park stands four miles from Stratford-upon-Avon. Nowadays the deer have run wild and can be seen roaming the highways and byways between Stratford and Charlecote. Four centuries ago however they were the target of many a bold poacher.

'On thy feet!'
The command was barked out across the rich grassland of Charlecote Park and the three men froze in the act of trussing a deer. They had spent a long cold night silently tracking it down, but not silently enough, for they in turn had been tracked by Sir Thomas Lucy's keepers.

The keepers came lumbering out of the night towards them. Dropping the half-trussed animal, the three poachers took to their heels and fled. They reached the ditch bordering the park, and this was their undoing. Two pitched forwards and fell headlong into the rich Warwickshire mud and within moments the keepers were upon them. The third poacher cleared the bank on the opposite side and disappeared into the night. The keepers tightened their grip on their two captives.
'God rot you and Sir Thomas!'
The older of the two thieves received a vicious back-hander in payment for his oath. He spat out a tooth and continued:
'I say God rot him and his fancy laws!'
The hand lashed out a second time and felled him to the ground. His companion, his beard tipped with Charlecote clay and his high forehead caked in mud, gazed myopically about him. One of the keepers nudged him none too gently.
'We'll see what Sir Thomas has to say about your evening's business my fine lad!'

Together they were dragged towards Charlecote House. Sir Thomas was in poor humour, his rightful slumber having been interrupted to deal with petty thieves. The two miscreants were dragged into the light and Sir Thomas cast his eye over them. A flicker of recognition passed over his face.

'You!' He thrust a fat finger towards the young man. 'Are you not the master-glover's son from Stratford?'

He turned to his servant.

'This kid-skin pair was his father's handiwork. This yearling delivered it to me himself!' He poked the boy hard in the ribs. 'So this is how you would repay me? Steal my deer eh?'

The youth peered short-sightedly about the room. The mud had dried on his forehead and he looked a pitiful sight.

'Take them to the gates, give them a sound whipping and send them on their way!' Sir Thomas gave the boy a final poke.

'And tell your father that my gloves shall be from Banbury henceforth!'

Sir Thomas swept back into the Hall. The keepers grinned vindictively as they pushed the unfortunate couple through the gates and waited while one of their number was sent for the leather thong that was to impart the lesson. The whipping having been carried out, the man and the boy staggered out into the road and began the long trek back to Stratford. They were on Clopton Bridge before either had the breath to speak.

'Dick Hart, I swear to you that I shall teach that old molligolliard a lesson he won't forget!' exclaimed the boy.

Dick clutched the bridge for support.

'If you know what's good for you you'll let sleeping dogs lie. Sir Thomas is a powerful man. It will do your father or yourself no good to aggravate him further. We were caught red-handed. Be glad we escaped with a whipping. Like I said, God rot him and his new law that sends honest folk like us out poaching!'

His young companion shook his head.

'I shall have the last laugh, wait and see!'

The two men walked into the town and went their separate ways. The young man made his way to his father's house in Henley Street. Married three years, and still unable to provide his wife with a home of her own. He carefully stepped over a stinking dunghill.

No doubt there would be a sharp tongue ready to lash him over his appearance and that night's escapade.

'I have to put up with your scribbling, and now this!' she would scold him. He paused. His scribbling, as she called it, would give him the revenge he sought. He let himself into the house and in the early morning gathered together his writing implements. Time enough before the rest of the household was awake.

A few hours later he was already across Clopton Bridge, through Alveston and on the road to Charlecote. Reaching the gates of Sir Thomas Lucy's home he drew from under his doublet a neatly penned script which he rapidly affixed to the gates before hurrying back onto the Stratford road.

It was not long before a waggoner from the estate halted at the gates, and scratching his head, ripped down the manuscript and delivered it to the House.

> *A parliament member, a justice of the peace,*
> *At home a poor scarecrow, at London an asse;*
> *If lousie is Lucy, as some folke miscalle it,*
> *Then Lucy is lousie, whatever befalle it.*
> *He thinks himself greate,*
> *Yet an asse in his state,*
> *We allowe by his eares but with asses to mate:*
> *If Lucy is lousie, as some folke miscalle it,*
> *Sing lousie Lucy, whatever befalle it.'*

Dick Hart wagged his finger at his young friend. They sat in the ale-house near Shottery, and both had quaffed freely of the rough, home-brewed cider. 'And now you've done it and no mistake! Sir Thomas is set on revenge for your fancy balladry! It'll be best for all concerned if you left Stratford with all haste!' The young man nodded his agreement. Dissatisfaction with this rural life had eaten into his soul some months ago. This would be the final push he needed.

He returned home to Henley Street, and bundling up his few clothes, and with a tearful farewell from his wife and family, Master William Shakespeare, apprentice glove-maker, poacher and scribbler of verses, set off for London to seek his fortune.

Shakespeare did not forget his encounter with Sir Thomas Lucy. His quest for revenge led him to base the character of Mr Justice Shallow in 'The Merry Wives of Windsor' on his old enemy, and he brings in several pointed asides regarding poached venison, and escaping without 'kissing the keeper's daughter'.

To be immortalised by Shakespeare might seem a great honour to many. Not so for one family. It is interesting to note that at one time the copy of the 'The Merry Wives of Windsor' that lay on the shelves of the library at Charlecote House had the scene with Justice Shallow ripped out.

THE GHOST BATTLE OF EDGEHILL

It was the 23rd December 1642, two months after the Battle of Edgehill. Some local shepherds and travellers, finding themselves on that hillside, were witnesses to an apparition of 'two jarring and contrary armies'. Such visions have been seen up to the present day, and few local folk will take it on themselves to walk along the escarpment on the anniversary of the battle. If they did, they reasoned, they might meet with Prince Rupert, galloping at the head of the Royalist forces, seeking the place where he was struck down.

Between midnight and one o'clock in the morning two travellers out of Banbury and a group of shepherds guarding their flock up on the Edge were halted in their business by the far-off sounds of drum and trumpet. The travellers from Banbury paid little heed, but the shepherds, being local men, were all too familiar with the sounds since it was a mere two months since the ghastly slaughter on that very hillside.

The shepherds began to pick out the cries of soldiers between the harsh call of the trumpets and the muffled beat of the drums, and as they listened the cries began to change, now sounding as if they were the last groans of the dying. The noises drew nearer and the frightened shepherds tried to run away, but the moment they tried to make their escape, the soldiers who were making the dreadful clamour appeared before them in the sky, with ensigns displayed. The shepherds were suddenly surrounded by the noise of cannon, drum and trumpet, and were unable to move for fear of being captured or killed by these infernal soldiers.

Until three in the morning they watched the ghastly battle, as time after time the two armies gave charge. At last the army carrying the King's Colours withdrew, the other army remaining for a short while as masters of the field and letting out cries of triumph. Then the soldiers, with all their drums, trumpets and flags, also vanished.

When they had recovered their wits the shepherds hurried to Kineton and the house of Mr William Wood, a Justice of the Peace, and to the house of Samuel Marshall, the Minister. At first scant attention was paid to such a tale, weight being given to the festive time of year and the likelihood of strong drink having played a part in the creation of this wondrous apparition. However, one of the shepherds being known to the Minister as a serious and sober man, swore on his oath to such an effect that it was decided that the following night, being Christmas Eve, the Justice of the Peace and the Minister, together with other village worthies, would travel to Edgehill to seek evidence of these scenes.

Soon after their arrival the sounds began again and they too were treated to the vision of phantom armies in combat. The gentlemen of the village, terrified out of their wits, fled screaming down the turnpike road back to Kineton and hid themselves in their houses, beseeching God to defend them from such hellish armies.

On the following Saturday the ghostly battle was seen again and many who saw it were so affected that they moved away from the area. The Minister, now convinced more than ever as to the terrible nature of the apparition, journeyed to Oxford to seek an audience with the King. On hearing his account the King immediately sent six of his most trusted officers to investigate. Meanwhile a further group of villagers had visited the hillside and had observed the visions. On returning to the local inn they were ridiculed by their more sceptical friends. But that same night the whole village was awakened by the sound of drums and the screams of the wounded and dying. Those brave enough to peer from their windows saw armed horsemen engage their enemy and then vanish into thin air.

The King's officers, arriving on the scene, took down many first-hand accounts from the villagers, and wasted no time in making their way up to the hillside themselves. They had not long to wait. Soon the sounds of the phantom armies began to echo across the headland and the full panoply of war materialised before them.

The officers returned to report to their King as broken men, for only two months before they themselves had fought at Edgehill, and during the long night, as they watched the fortunes of the ghostly armies ebb and flow, they recognised the faces of many of their dead companions who had been slain during the encounter.

CLOPTON HOUSE

Clopton House, one mile from Stratford-upon-Avon, has a dark history. It has connections both with Shakespeare and the Gunpowder Plot. The tragic story of Charlotte Clopton is said to have provided Shakespeare with the ending to 'Romeo and Juliet' and furnished Edgar Allan Poe with the plot for 'The Fall of the House of Usher'. Part of 'The Taming of the Shrew' was set in the great dining room of the house.

In 1564, the year of Shakespeare's birth, the Great Plague spread across the country and laid claim to its first Warwickshire victims. All strangers were forbidden entry into Stratford-upon-Avon, and the inhabitants were ordered not to leave. The town council met in the open air for fear of infection.

Charlotte Clopton was one of the first in Stratford to fall sick. Rumour had it that she had recently cut a root of white bryony in the gardens of the house, a sign of ill-omen. The dreaded black pustules formed rapidly on her body and within hours she was dead. Burial was a matter of urgency to prevent contagion and so, with the minimum of ceremony, Charlotte's body was taken to Holy Trinity Church, where Shakespeare was later to be interred. Here she was placed in the family vault in the Chapel of Our Lady the Virgin.

The plague continued to seek out fresh victims, and within a fortnight another member of the Clopton family succumbed to the ghastly buboes. Again the burial was a swift affair, and the family vault was quickly re-opened. Within it was revealed a sight so terrible as to cause the strongest to fall back and retch in horror.

Charlotte Clopton's coffin lay open, and her body stood upright against the wall of the vault. Her finger ends were ripped to shreds and locked against the stonework in her last desperate attempts to secure her freedom from her tomb. On one shoulder was a terrible wound where she had turned and bitten into herself in her last terrible anguish.

Her ghost returned to Clopton House to join the spirit of a priest who haunts the upper reaches of the building. He was murdered there and dragged along the landing to a bedroom before being hurled ignominiously into the moat below. A thin black line traces the path of the body and it is said that this is a bloodstain that no amount of cleaning can ever erase.

In 1605, Ambrose Rookwood, a young man who had already been prosecuted for harbouring priests, lived at the house. Rookwood was a quiet, devout man who became involved in the Gunpowder Plot only because of his friendship with Robert Catesby. Many of the old Catholic families in Warwickshire were aware that some plot was in progress, and a great party of such men, armed to the teeth, supposedly for a day's hunting, gathered at the home of Sir Everard Digby at Dunchurch, some twenty miles from Stratford. They were ready to follow up the success of events in London with an uprising in the Midlands. However the plot was betrayed and the leaders fled from London to Warwickshire in the hope that these influential Catholics might yet be roused to continue the revolt. It was not to be and the leaders were left without support. They rode to Warwick, where they helped themselves to fresh horses from the castle itself and attacked and overcame a party mustered by the Sherriff.

Through Snitterfield they rode, and came at last to Stratford, where, in the Market Square, they sounded a trumpet and made a stirring speech aimed at drawing recruits from the townspeople. Few dared to show their faces around their doors however. No further support was obtained from the surrounding villages, and disheartened they made their way through Alcester and out of Warwickshire, to meet their fate.

THE SLEEPING SWEEPS OF WARWICKSHIRE

Jeremy Nollykins was the meanest, richest sweep in Warwickshire. He owed his wealth to the unstinted efforts of his three young apprentices. But Nollykins' desire for even more money eventually backfired.

Jeremy Nollykins, Master Sweep by Appointment to the Mayor and Corporation and the Lords of three local Manors, was the meanest man in Warwickshire. Having indulged himself in too much good food and strong ale as a result of his thriving business, he was now too fat and sluggish to burden himself with the messy side of his work. This he left to three poor, half-starved apprentices. It was these poor souls who had to climb up from sooty brick to sooty brick and sweep until their hands and faces were blistered and scorched and their knees rubbed raw from gaining a precarious hold on the inside of the chimneys. Sometimes they would get jammed, or lose their grip and plummet into the fireplace below, together with a great cloud of soot. Nollykins beat them unmercifully when this happened, as his clients were somewhat averse to soot-covered rooms.

Nollykins, or Old Noll as he was generally known, supervised the collection of money, which he tied up in fat leather bags. However, none of his wealth was frittered away on his three apprentices. Watery gruel for breakfast and supper was their staple diet. Occasionally, when he felt particularly generous, he treated them to a pudding with pale gobbets of suet floating in a thin gravy. On Saturdays however he usually prepared a veritable feast for the starving lads: Pease pudding and pottage. This by no means indicated a change of heart by Old Noll; the boys owed their good fortune to the fact that Saturday was the day the Mayor looked in to check that the boys were being well fed and cared for.

Despite all these privations the boys were a merry trio, and any spare time they had was spent cavorting around the woods, scrabbling up and down the quarry or swimming in the river.

Nollykins disliked them finding any pleasure in life and beat them regularly in a vain attempt to subdue their high spirits, but he never beat them as hard as he would have liked – after all he had to keep them fit enough to do his dirty work. He would have liked to have saved even more money on their board too but the wretches required at least some food to keep them alive. On many an evening Old Noll would make his way up to the old attic where the three boys slept, covered with filthy old sacking. Seeing dream-smiles on their faces, he would fly into a rage, and his fingers would itch to beat them for daring to sleep so happily, but he knew that you must never beat a dreamer.

One night Old Noll was unable to sleep, and slipping downstairs he let himself out into the street to take a midnight walk. It had been a warm summer's day and reaching the outskirts of the village Old Noll sat himself down and turned his face towards the evening breeze. As he sat there his ears caught the distant sounds of music and singing. He listened more intently and gradually he was able to make out the sound of children's voices. Suddenly, streaming out from the village came a horde of children, skipping and dancing towards him. As they danced by, Old Noll noticed something very curious about them. Not one footstep could be heard and their expressions were dream-like and waxen. Scarcely had he taken this in, when, to his absolute astonishment his own three apprentices came skipping and dancing past him, snapping their fingers and waving their arms in time to the ghostly music.

As soon as the children had disappeared Old Noll swiftly made his way back to his house. He climbed the narrow stairs to the attic and peered inside. There, lying fast asleep, were his apprentices.

Over the next few months Old Noll followed the boys' dream spirits as they left the attic and joined those of the other village children in their games, and each morning, on his return, he would find their earthly bodies wrapped in peaceful slumber, a happy smile upon their faces. Now very close to Old Noll's house lived a witch and eventually he sought her counsel. The old woman offered to help and they haggled before agreeing a good price for her assistance. At last he thrust a grubby crown coin into her hand.

The crone spat on it and spoke: 'Wake a Sleeper before his dream spirit has returned to his body and it is sudden death!,' she advised, 'But', and here she paused meaningfully, 'keep the dream spirit out without waking the body and that body will be your slave forever, and furthermore will never age!'

Old Noll leaned forward eagerly at this news. Here was his chance to increase his fortune without paying a further penny for his apprentices' keep!
'Tell me', he asked, 'what must I do to keep their dream spirits and their bodies apart?'
'A horseshoe hung upside down outside their door will suffice', replied the witch. 'Walls are like smoke to these spirits, but they cannot stand the thought of iron.'
Now the advice she gave Old Noll was only partly true, for she had as little love for him as did his apprentices.

Nollykins returned home and began to make his preparations. The next day was St. Nicholas's Day and snow lay deep on the ground. At the stroke of midnight Old Noll crept from his house and took up his position at the end of the street. Sure enough the familiar strains of music began to fill the air, and flitting through the darkness came the village children, followed by his three apprentices.

Old Noll ran back into the boys' attic room and swiftly hammered an up-ended horseshoe to their door. He laughed silently as he carefully opened the door a few inches. There were the sleeping forms of the three boys.
'You're mine for ever, lads!' he gloated, and sped downstairs to celebrate his good fortune with a massive supper.

The following morning, as he prepared some gruel, he whistled to himself in sheer delight. Noticing that the boys were late in rising he reached for his stick and softly climbed the stairs. To his horror the boys lay there, but this time no dream-smile played across their lips, and their faces had changed to the colour of grey stone. Old Noll knew he dare not wake them, and that they themselves would never wake of their own accord. The witch had deceived him!

He ran into the street cursing her name. A doctor was summoned. And pronounced an advanced state of catalepsy and that they would only awake when God willed it.

For allowing the apprentices to fall into such a parlous state of health, the Mayor fined Old Noll five hundred guineas. Nollykins was so confused by this turn of events that he clear forgot to take down the horseshoe. Eventually the three young sweeps were removed to the local museum and placed in a great glass case with a frame of solid Warwickshire oak. And there, in the upstairs room of the museum, the three boys slumbered on.

Old Noll eventually went to meet his Maker and for fifty years the three apprentices lay in their glass and oak coffin. Then, one day, the curator of the museum, who for all those years had not failed to visit the boys and give their case a daily dusting, fell ill. His niece, a beautiful young girl, was sent to show visitors around the museum. Little did she know, as she removed the key from the glass case to take a look inside, that by removing the small piece of iron, she had broken the witch's spell. As she placed the key carefully in her pocket she unknowingly removed the barrier between the sleeping forms and their dream spirits. There was a terrible crash of glass, and leaping from their tomb came the three apprentices. Out of the museum they ran and through the village and into the distance, laughing and singing as they had done so all those years ago. The whole village was summoned to search for the boys but from that day to this they have never been seen again.

THE ROLLRIGHT STONES

Long Compton has been noted for its witches since ancient times. It was said there were enough witches in the village to draw a load of hay up Long Compton Hill. The witches of Long Compton have long been associated with the Rollright Stones, a stone circle on the Warwickshire-Oxfordshire border.

When Rollo the Dane was about to invade England, a prophet whispered to him the following words:

> *'When Long Compton you shall see,*
> *You shall King of England be'*

The Dane, together with his Knights and his army, marched upon Long Compton and eventually made camp just beyond the headland that overlooks the village. There was intrigue in the camp, and certain of the Knights withdrew a little distance and gathered together in a huddle to plot the downfall of Rollo. Unaware of their plotting Rollo prepared to march the final steps to the ridge which would win him sight of Long Compton and the throne of England. Before he could do so however one of the village witches stepped forward and spoke:

> *'As Long Compton thou canst not see*
> *King of England thou shalt not be.*
> *Rise up stick and stand thou stone*
> *For King of England thou shall be none*
> *You and your men hoar-stones shall be*
> *And I myself an eldern tree'*

They were instantly transformed into stone, the King becoming a giant stone, the King Stone, which stands to this day just beneath the ridge a mere half a dozen steps beyond the view of Long Compton.

For many years an elder tree grew entwined against the King Stone, and on certain wintry afternoons, when the sun is low on the horizon, the contorted features of the monarch who never was can be plainly seen. The bulk of his army formed a tight circle of some seventy stones just a few hundred yards beyond, and half a mile away to the east, in a nearby field, the larger shapes of the Whispering Knights still crouch in the act of plotting against their King.

Many legends have sprung up concerning the Stones. It is said to this day that they cannot be counted twice and the number made to tally. If pierced with a knife they will bleed, and no gate on the way up to the circle will ever stay shut.

In the 1800s a farmer by the name of Hugh Boffin decided to move the King Stone down to his farm in the village in order to bridge a culvert on his land. His team of horses was eight strong and yet he was unable to draw the King Stone far down the hill. The team broke into a malt sweat and pulled and kicked as if they were terrified. Farmer Boffin gave in and unharnessed the team, as he thought it as well that the King Stone be returned to its rightful place. As he unharnessed them the last horse broke free and succeeded in dragging the gigantic bulk of the King Stone back up the hill without further assistance.

In recent years signs of witch-fires have often been found at the centre of the circle, and it would be a foolhardy person who ventured near the Stones on All Hallow's Eve.

THE RED HORSE OF TYSOE

"And Tysoe's wondrous theme, the martial horse,
Carved on the yielding turf, armorial sign of Hengist,
Saxon Chief! Studious to preserve
The favr'ite form, the treach'rous conquerors,
Their vassal tribes compel with festive rites
Its fading figure yearly to renew
And to the neighb'ring vale imparts its name"

Reverend Jago, 'Edgehill'

On Palm Sunday 1461, Richard Neville, Earl of Warwick, led his men into the bloodiest battle of the War of the Roses: The Battle of Towton Field. His army found themselves in particularly perilous circumstances and so the Earl ordered his horse to be brought to him, and pausing only to kiss the hilt of his sword, plunged the weapon deep into the gallant charger's side. As he did so he vowed to meet the enemy on equal terms with his humblest foot-soldiers. Such was the feeling of devotion aroused in his men that a notable victory was secured.

It is said that a retainer of the Earl returned to the village of Tysoe, and, inspired by the Earl's brave gesture, ordered the cutting out of the figure of a giant horse on the hillside above the village in commemoration of the event. The finished creature measured, according to the antiquary Sir William Dugdale, 'from croup to chest thirty-four feet, from the shoulder to the ears fourteen feet, from the ears to the nose seven feet six inches, and from the shoulder to the ground sixteen feet or fifty-seven hands.'

Most local people know for a fact that there have been two Red Horses. In 1800, the landlord of the Sunrising Inn ploughed up the original Red Horse and cut out a smaller one in Sunrise Covert. The site of the original figure was forgotten and the site of the second Red Horse is now covered by trees.

What is not generally realised is that there were in fact not two but five Red Horses. Investigations carried out by W. G. Miller and K. A. Carrdus in the nineteen-sixties, involving aerial photographs, revealed three horses cut into the slope known as 'The Hangings'.

The first, an enormous galloping horse, nearly 100 yards long and 70 yards wide must have been the original figure. A second figure, about two thirds the size stood just in front of the first, and a third, small figure about 18 yards long and with short legs faced in the opposite direction. This third horse was the last true Red Horse of Tysoe, and the one ploughed up by Simon Nicholls when he bought Sunrising Farm from the Marquess of Northampton in 1800. Until this time there had been an obligation on the part of the farm workers to scour the figure annually, but the new owner, by ploughing it up, put an end to this tradition.

Unfortunately the event, over the years, had taken on the form of a Palm Sunday jollification, and the new landlord suffered greatly from the loss of cakes and ale. The following year he shrewdly decided to carve a new figure in order to restore his profits, but Miller and Carrdus describe this as only seventeen feet long and 'showing a happily inebriated pantomime horse with human feet'. The annual scouring was never revived.

The final Red Horse is said to have been cut out of Spring Hill by a Mr Savory at the turn of the last century. Sadly he became so annoyed by the number of visitors who trampled across his land to view it that he deliberately ploughed it over in 1910.

As to the origins of the first Red Horse of Tysoe, there are many people who feel that this goes back far further than the time of Richard Neville. The name Tysoe is said to derive from 'Tiw's-Ho' or 'The spur of hillside dedicated to the Saxon god Tiw.' Was then the first Red Horse a relic of more ancient festivals and magic rituals to ensure fertility and good crops?

LADY GODIVA

Leofric, Earl of Mercia, ruled over a great part of the Midlands in the tenth century, and, with his wife Godiva, he founded an abbey in Coventry. But it is for Godiva's famous ride that the couple are best remembered.

Godiva, or to give her her proper name – Godgifu or 'gift of God', was a woman of notable beauty and purity, with hair that was fair and long. Greatly concerned for the people of Coventry, she longed for them to be spared the heavy tolls and taxes of that time and on their behalf she pleaded many times with her husband Leofric. Annoyed by her persistent nagging he eventually answered: 'Mount your horse naked and ride through the market of the town from the beginning to the end where people are assembled, and when you return you shall have your wish.'
'And if I am willing to do this,' replied Godiva, 'do you give me leave?'
'I do,' answered Leofric.

So Lady Godiva, attended by two soldiers, prepared to ride naked. However, before commencing her ride she visited the magistrates of the city and told them of how she planned to rid them of their burden of taxes, but out of reverence for her womanhood she asked if a commandment could be sent before the time of her journey, telling everyone to stay in their homes and to shut their windows. No-one was to so much as look out onto the street until she had safely passed by.

This undertaking having been given, she mounted her horse, and letting down her golden tresses so that her whole body was covered apart from her legs, she rode through the town unseen. Her ride completed, Leofric was as good as his word and freed the people from taxes, all except the toll on horses, and in a charter under his own seal he granted relief to poor traders visiting the town.

By the seventeenth century the story began to be told that not all of townsfolk had deferred to Godiva's wishes.

It was said that one man named Tom, a tailor, heard Godiva's horse whinny as it passed his house. Letting down a window he spied Lady Godiva and was struck blind. A poem by H. W. Hawkes, performed before Queen Victoria in 1842, recounts the tale:

'O Tom how couldst thou act so rude
To lady chaste and kind?
It proves thou wast of wicked heart
Likewise ungrateful mind.
But hadst thou known thy precious sight
Would the sad forfeit be,
Thy rashness ne'er had prompted thee
To peep at this lady.'

A wooden figure, carved around 1600, with sightless eyes and a ghastly face, is said to be that of 'Peeping Tom'. It was kept originally at the house of Alderman Owen at Greyfriars Lane but then stood in the Leofric Hotel in the centre of Coventry until the hotel closed in 2009. From 1658 a representation of Lady Godiva provided the main attraction at the Coventry Great Fair, and in the nineteenth century the actresses taking the part began to appear in scantier and scantier costumes, much to the delight of the audiences.

One year there were wild rumours that the following year she would appear 'clad as the original'. Such was the strength of these rumours that the local clergy became involved and heated exchanges occurred between the Mayor and the Bishop. One vicar was so incensed at the thought of such a lewd display that he packed some additional trimmings in his bag and hurried to St. Mary's Hall, where he intended to add to the lady's dress should it prove unsuitable. As the Godiva of that year, a cheerful music-hall artiste, struggled into her miniscule costume, she was confronted by the irate clergyman. She cried 'Why bless you man, I've never had so many clothes on in my life!'

SIR GUY OF WARWICK AND THE DUN COW

Sir Guy is said to have lived in Saxon times during the reign of King Athelstan. He set out from Warwick to win fame in heathen lands and his exploits included the slaying of Dragons, Giants and Sultans. But perhaps his most renowned adventure was his battle with the dread Dun Cow at Dunsmore Heath.

'Mother! Mother! The cow is here again!'
The child's mother wiped her grimy hands on her greasy apron and hurried outside. Sure enough the large brown cow was peacefully munching the grass on the edge of Dunsmore Heath.
'Are we going to milk it again?' inquired the child.
The mother paused a moment and her eyes sparkled.
'Go get your father. Tell him it is here again. The cow that gave us milk the time before.'
The child ran off. Soon the mother had collected all the containers that she could lay hands on. The child returned with her father, who cast one eye on the giant cow and then slipped inside the hut. He emerged clasping a large makeshift sieve.
'Quickly, before it goes away again. This trick will keep us well supplied, never fear!'

They crept up to the cow, who gazed good-naturedly at them from over its shoulder. The man stationed himself comfortably beneath the cow's udders and whilst the child kept it satisfied with fresh clumps of grass, he began to milk it into the sieve. His wife held each container in turn beneath the sieve. Occasionally the cow glanced back, but noticing that the sieve remained empty, as sieves do, it continued to give her milk. Soon all the containers were full.
'It seems a pity that others cannot benefit from our good fortune,' reasoned the man. He summoned the child.

'Run and hence and tell good neighbour Albertus of our find. Tell him to bring as many containers as he can, and hurry before the creature wanders away again.'

Soon Albertus and family arrived and filled all their containers in a like manner. Again the sieve was put to good use, and the cow, noting it still remained empty, gave its milk.

'This is good magic and should rightly be shared with others,' Albertus declared. 'I shall tell all our neighbours on our way home. Let them come and share our good fortune!'

By dusk a great line of men and women waited patiently for their turn to milk the Dun Cow, and it seemed that as long as the sieve appeared empty then there was enough milk for all. As darkness gathered and the last few village folk awaited their turn, the cow gazed down, seemingly through the sieve. It was as if it suddenly realised the deception that had been practised on it. The cow gave a tremendous kick, severing the head of the poor unfortunate who was grasping its udders, and leaping forward it began to trample and gore the villagers. Women and children were mangled under its hooves, and their frail bodies ripped open by its fearsome horns. Eventually, sated for the moment of its blood-lust, the monster disappeared into the darkness towards a dense thicket on the edge of the Heath. No doubt it wanted to plot its further revenge on the greedy folk who had all but exhausted its milk.

From that day a reign of terror was visited on that part of Warwickshire. Over the following weeks and months hundreds perished at the horns of the Dun Cow. No one dared wander abroad at night and in the darkness the maddened bellowing of the enraged creature echoed for miles around. It was not long before the King, who was then in York, heard of this terrible visitation. He pondered long upon the problem, and eventually offered a knighthood and other privileges to anyone brave enough to undertake to destroy the Dun Cow. However, so great was the terror that had spread throughout the country concerning the monster that not one person came forward.

The King lamented the fact that the one man in England brave enough to face the creature, Guy of Warwick, was in France, embarking on fresh quests to win the hand of his heart's desire. Fortunately the King was wrong, and Guy had been unable to cross to France because of contrary winds. Hearing of the Dun Cow, Guy resolved to destroy the creature. He took with him his sword, his strongest battle axe and his bow and quiver. Riding hard he eventually reached that part of Dunsmore Heath where the monster had last been seen. Here was a great thicket of trees near a pool of stagnant water. As Guy rode along he saw the terrible signs of the beast's ravages. There were the bodies of men torn open and rotting in the sun, and carcasses of woodland animals gored almost to nothingness. Seeing these terrible sights filled Guy with a great anger at the deeds of the Dun Cow.

At last he came across the monster. It spied Guy first and thrusting its head through the trees it emitted a tremendous bellow. Twelve feet high it stood, and eighteen feet in length, its sharp horns stained with the gore of its victims. Guy reached for his bow and let fly an arrow which ricocheted back as if it had struck a wall of iron. Flinching from this attack, the Dun Cow now ran towards him, its horns lowered for the charge. Guy lifted high his battle axe and struck the maddened creature on the forehead. It recoiled and with a hideous roar gave charge again. This time its horns locked against his armour and dented the breastplate. Pulling himself free Guy smote the animal a desperate blow under the ear, the only place where it could be wounded. The blow was mortal and leaping upon the dying animal he hewed at it until, with a terrible groan, it died. In its death throes the blood coursed from its neck, staining the ground and the waters of the stagnant pool nearby. Guy immediately rode to the nearest town and announced the monster's death.

The King summoned Guy to York, and after feasting him, dubbed him Sir Guy in honour of his brave deed. A rib from the monster was then taken with due ceremony to hang in Warwick Castle, and Sir Guy departed to take ship for fresh adventures in far-off lands.

MOLL BLOXHAM OF WARWICK CASTLE

**'Milk and butter I sell ever
Weight and measure I give never'**

Moll Bloxham, an ancient retainer at Warwick Castle, was at long last given permission to sell for her own gain some of the surplus milk and butter not needed by the Earl of Warwick and his family. To help her even further she was allowed to trade from the castle's Caesar's Tower.

It was not long before word began to get back to the Earl that Moll was short-changing her customers. For a while he let sleeping dogs lie, but eventually the outcry became so great that he decided that a gentle word should be had with the old crone. Despite his mild warning she continued to give short measure in her dealings with the townsfolk, and with some considerable regret the Earl was forced to withdraw both the supply of milk and butter and the use of the tower. The day after these privileges were withdrawn Moll Bloxham disappeared. Many of the disgruntled townsfolk muttered of supernatural aid, her opportune disappearance removing her from the necessity of answering the awkward questions of many cheated customers. Within days of her disappearance however, the Earl's family became aware of a large black dog roaming the castle. It was soon accepted that this animal was the late unlamented Moll Bloxham. Eventually the Earl was persuaded to have this spirit exorcised, and called upon three members of the clergy to carry it out. At first their combined efforts were to no avail, but at last the great dog was cornered in the very tower where the thieving hag had plied her trade. Face to face with the priests, the monstrous hound sprang from Caesar's Tower into the river far below and was caught within a chamber contrived beneath the fletcher dam. A statue of Moll was afterwards placed on the tower to mark the place where she leapt to her doom. This statue performed a useful function in later years, acting as a 'watcher', fooling any enemies who might try to take the castle by surprise into believing a sentinel was watching from the ramparts.

JEREMIAH STONE AND THE DEVIL

The Battle of Edgehill on 23rd October 1642, the first general engagement between Royalist and Parliamentary armies, re-introduced the horrors of civil war to England after an interval of one hundred and fifty years. It is not surprising that the surrounding villages are rich in stories of the supernatural consequences of the battle.

As the noise of battle died away, one certain Jeremiah Stone, a corporal of dragoons, seized his chance to loot the body of a King's Messenger on the field of battle. Behind him fifteen hundred men lay dead and awaiting burial in mass graves along the Kineton road.

Stone quickly realised that his only hope of escaping with the loot was to reach the safety of Kineton village. He had already been set upon once during the course of the battle, by a pikeman who had succeeded in wounding him in the arm. In turn, Jeremiah Stone relieved him of the cares of this life. On reaching Kineton, Stone made his way to the Anchor Inn, where the landlord was not averse to coming to the aid of either faction should the price be right. A hasty deal was entered into, involving shelter, treatment for his wound and safe-keeping for his loot. After several days his strength had revived sufficiently for him to accost the landlord with a view to retrieving his illicit wealth. At this demand the wily landlord denied all such knowledge of the arrangement and summoned his serving wench, who rather too hastily agreed with her master. At this Stone went berserk. He drew his sword and tried to break down the door but within moments was arrested on a charge of breaking and entering, and was thrown into Warwick jail. He languished for many weeks in the dark recesses of the prison. One evening his dulled senses alerted him to the sounds of the cell door being unlocked. Stone peered into the gloom, hoping for a fresh supply of food and water. Imagine his horror when he was confronted by none other than the Devil. During that long night Stone entered into a hideous pact. Help and revenge in exchange for his soul.

The morning of the trial dawned and Stone was arraigned in court, the Devil's instructions fresh in his mind; 'Choose for your attorney the man wearing a red cap and feather.'

Stone took this advice and soon his lawyer called upon the landlord of the Anchor Inn to give his evidence. The landlord took the stand and the lawyer suggested that his inn should be searched to settle once and for all the matter of the missing treasure. At this suggestion the landlord became much agitated and cried out:

'I am a man of honour! I refuse to submit to such a demand from a common criminal. I have given my oath that I took no valuables from this man. The Devil take me if I tell a lie!'

A hush fell over the court and before the assembled crowd Stone's attorney rose to his feet. Gone was his red cap and feather. There before the courtroom stood the Devil himself. With a goat-like bound the Arch-fiend vaulted the witness stand and seized the hapless landlord and threw him over his shoulder. The couple made their way swiftly into the market place, and as the members of the court spilled out into the street to follow their progress the Devil and his prize disappeared into thin air, leaving nothing but a sulphurous stench.

As for Jeremiah Stone, no one really knows. Some said that he returned to Kineton to retrieve his loot but that it could not be found. Others say that he died, deranged, a short time after the trial, the Devil being keen to exact his side of the bargain.

THE BURNING OF MARY CLUES

Human combustion is a terrifying and little recorded supernatural occurrence. In Coventry, over three hundred years ago, Mary Clues met such a grisly end and found her way into medical history.

Mary Clues emptied her half-pint mug of rum and belched resonantly. Her one solace and escape from miserable, bone-grinding poverty was her addiction to ardent spirits. She gazed about bleary eyed and summoned the pot boy to replenish her mug, this time with an astringent concoction of aniseed cordial. In the last year of her life scarcely a day passed in which she did not consume at least this measure of rot-gut.

Soon however the raw alcohol had so ravaged her liver and other vital organs that she was confined to her bed, unable to reach the haven of the hostelry a few doors along the street. She lay abed in her squalid hovel, a single rush-light illuminating her drab surroundings.

On the last evening of her life she lay listening to the street noises until she fell into a fitful slumber. The next morning a slim tendril of smoke was seen twisting its way out of her window. Two burly neighbours rushed upstairs and broke down the door, only to be met by a sudden sheet of white flame which flared for a moment and then was gone.

Between the bed and the chimney-place lay the remains of Mary Clues. Of her body, only one leg and thigh were still entire and nothing whatsoever remained of her muscles or internal viscera. On closer examination the skin, her breasts, the bones of her skull and spine were entirely calcined and covered with a strange white efflorescence. Strangest of all was the fact that the meagre furnishings and possessions of the old crone were untouched and apart from a blackened human silhouette-like imprint on the wall nothing in the room except the body showed any trace of fire.

48

The accident was reported to the Annual Registrar by Mr Willmer, a surgeon of the city of Coventry, and his report encouraged a Dr Trotter to research the happening. In his essay 'On Drunkenness', Dr Trotter attested that 'several such instances had occurred throughout the land, the victims of such spontaneous combustion always being inordinately addicted to strong drink, and always females of advanced age.'

The interested reader may be referred to the pages of the 'Pathologic Anatomy of Man' in the 'Encyclopaedia Methodique', but as Dugdale remarked: 'The habitual drunkard is seldom inquisitive, or perhaps the frightful details there given of spontaneous combustion might reclaim him from the horrid practice.'

DOCTOR WELCHMAN OF KINETON

A noted character in Kineton about 180 years ago was Edward Welchman, a doctor whose practice ranged from Warwick to Banbury. He was very fond of good dinners and fine wine, and was locally regarded as a brilliant man. Sometimes however he met his match.

One evening the good doctor was just about to leave his house to partake of what promised to be a particularly good dinner, when he was summoned to attend the wife of a local cow-leech who lived some few miles away. By dint of his skills the woman duly recovered. Soon after this the good doctor's cow fell ill and the cow-leech was sent for. After bringing his own special skills to bear he succeeded in curing the cow.

The doctor's bills were usually paid at the Statute Fair, or local 'Mop' as it was called thereabouts. A luncheon was provided in the doctor's dining room for the local farmers and a substantial dinner in the kitchen for his other patients.

After dinner the cow-leech presented himself at the doctor's study to settle his account, for he had by now received the doctor's bill for ministering to his spouse during her illness. The bill was rather large, but fair, considering the acknowledged prowess of Doctor Welchman.
'I have a little bill for you too,' said the cow-leech.
'Of course, of course,' replied the good doctor. 'Let me see it and I shall be glad to settle it forthwith.'
When the doctor saw it he opened his eyes wide, for the totals of the two bills were exactly the same.
'What do you mean by this?' complained the doctor. 'Your bill is as large as mine!'
'Well you see,' explained the cow-leech. 'I attended your cow just as many times as you yourself came to my old woman.'
'Now come, come my good man!' exclaimed the doctor. 'You cannot charge me as much for attending my cow as I charge for attending your wife.'

'Well, it be the same distance from your house to mine as it is from mine to yours,' reasoned the wily cow-leech.

'But it takes far more skill to cure a human being than to cure a cow!' cried the doctor.

'Begging your pardon,' said the cow-leech, 'but when you came to my old woman you asked her what were her simpletons, as you called 'em, and she told you. If I'd asked your cow what her simpletons were, would she have told me? No sir, it takes a deal more skill to cure a cow that to cure a human.'

The doctor paid the bill.

A further incident concerning Doctor Welchman is also recounted: One evening after a hard day's work the doctor returned home tired and hungry. He made a hearty meal and also took several glasses of fine red wine with it. Having just completed his splendid repast he was unexpectedly summoned to a patient who had suddenly been taken ill. Riding in the fresh air to the patient's home, the effects of the wine became more marked, and he was in a merry state when he arrived to examine his client. On reaching the patient's bedside he proceeded to feel for the pulse. However, by mistake he seized hold of his own wrist.

'Hah! All that is wrong with this man is that he is completely drunk!' he exclaimed.

This story soon spread throughout the neighbourhood, and might have been thought to have been detrimental to his professional reputation in the community. Not one bit! The local folk reasoned that if the old doctor, well in his cups, could accurately diagnose his own condition, then what powers he must have when sober!

SAINT AUGUSTINE VISITS LONG COMPTON

In the year 404 AD, Saint Augustine arrived in England to preach the Gospel. In the course of his travels he came to Long Compton. The strange effigy in the south porch of the village church is said to be of this holy man.

Saint Augustine had only recently arrived in the parish of Long Compton when he was approached by the parish priest, who sought his help over the delicate affair of the Lord of the Manor who would not pay his tithes. Saint Augustine listened to the priest's tale and having considered the matter decided to confront the wayward Lord on his next visit to the church.

When the occasion arose, Saint Augustine addressed the obstinate nobleman and demanded of him the reason for his refusal to pay his tithes.
'Know you not,' declared the Saint, 'that they are not yours but God's.'
To this the Knight replied:
'Did I not plough the land, and sow the land, and did I not in the fullness of time harvest the land? I will therefore have the tenth sheaf as well as the other nine!'
At this Saint Augustine cried out:
'If you will not pay then you shall be excommunicated!'
Hurrying to the altar he raised his hands and declared:
'I command that no excommunicated person be present at this Mass!'

No sooner were these words spoken when there came a dreadful moan from the churchyard outside. A corpse that lay buried at the entrance to the church had risen from the grave and had taken his place just beyond the confines of the churchyard. Saint Augustine completed his Mass and then, together with the terrified congregation and the errant Earl, he made his way to where the dead man stood. Saint Augustine was the first to speak.
'I command, in the name of God, that you tell me who you are.'
The dead man's rotting lips parted in reply.

52

'I was Patron of the place in the time of the Britons,' he whispered, and his voice was hoarse with the knowledge of all the terrors of the Pit.

'The Priest warned me yet never would I pay him my tithes, and so I died excommunicated and was thrust into Hell!'

On hearing this Saint Augustine ordered him to lead them to the place where this priest was buried. The spectre wasted no time in directing him to another grave.

'To the end that all men may know that life and death are in the hands of God, to whom nothing is impossible,' declared Saint Augustine, 'arise in His Name, for we have need of you.'

Slowly, from his ancient grave, the priest arose and stood before them. Saint Augustine turned to him, and raising his hand towards the other hapless corpse said:

'Brother, do you know this man?'

'Yes,' replied the long-dead priest. 'He was always a rebel to the Church, a withholder of his tithes, and even to the very last a wicked man, which caused me to excommunicate him.'

Saint Augustine replied, 'Brother, you know that God is merciful, so we must have pity of this miserable creature who has for so long endured the pains of Hell.'

Saint Augustine turned to see the wretched corpse upon its knees now blabbering for forgiveness and absolution.

'God is merciful!' cried Saint Augustine, and delivering to him a scourge, he granted absolution, and commanded that he return once more to his grave. The dead man reached his graveside and before the astounded congregation was immediately resolved to dust.

Saint Augustine now spoke to the ancient priest.

'How long have you been buried?'

'One hundred and fifty years,' was the reply.

'And how have you fared since then?' inquired the Saint.

'Very well,' replied the priest. 'I have enjoyed the delights of Eternal Life.'

'Tell me,' asked the Blessed Saint, 'should I pray to God that you may be returned to this life, so that by your preaching you may save many more souls?'

'I beg that you shall not disturb my quiet to bring me back to this troublesome world,' implored the priest.

'Very well, go on thy way and rest in peace,' declared Saint Augustine, and the priest, returning in the same manner to his grave, was also translated into dust.

Then Saint Augustine turned to the Lord of the Manor, who fell trembling and weeping at his feet.

'And now, my son,' demanded the Saint, 'will you pay the tithes you owe?'

The Lord of the Manor lay at his feet and confessed his sins and craved pardon. Henceforth he became a devout follower of Saint Augustine all the days of his life.

CONKERS

Many small hamlets in the south of the county still boast large manor houses which date back hundreds of years. This story is about one such place.

Billy Barnes carefully placed his fingers into a cow-pat and proudly withdrew a wizened conker. He wiped the surplus dirt against his trousers and polished the horse-chestnut until it gleamed.

'That'll be a twentier, bet yer any money!'

His friend nodded gravely.

'Where did you get it?'

'Down in the field opposite the Post Office.'

Billy pocketed the conker and pointed towards the old manor house that stood solidly at the bottom of the lane.

'Mind you, over that wall, that's where the best ones are!'

They both gazed at the high wall that surrounded the garden of the big house.

'See the horse chestnut tree growing there? Loaded it is. I bet any one of those would be hundreder. Given the right secret treatment that is!'

Billy was proud of his formula for hardening his champion conkers.

'How come no-one ever gets any conkers from the big house?' his friend inquired as they made their way down the lane.

'It's the Johnsons. Stuck up lot my Dad says. Don't want any kids around upsettin' their precious gardens. Been like that for years, My Dad says when he was a lad him and his mates couldn't get in there either.'

Billy paused at the foot of the wall of Cotswold stone.

'Mind you, I reckon….'

His friend butted in.

'You'd break your neck climbing up there!'

Billy shook his head.

'No, just look round the back. The wall's beginning to crumble with age. I reckon I could get enough hand-holds there to get to the top. It'd be dead easy from there onwards. I could get over onto one of the branches of the conker tree. Look, it overhangs just in the right place!'

'All the same,' continued his friend, 'I wouldn't like to risk it.'
Billy shrugged.
'With the right treatment one of those could be a world champion conker I reckon. Just look at the size of them!'
Billy's friend hopped nervously from one foot to the other.
'It's time I was getting home. My Mum gets upset if I'm late for tea.'
'Chicken!!'
Billy turned to examine the crumbling wall more closely. Small flakes of stone came away in his hand, but the rest of the wall stood as firm as it had done for the past four hundred years. Glancing around to make sure there was no one in sight apart from the disappearing figure of his friend, Billy carefully placed his boot into a crevice about two feet up the wall. Grasping a protruding stone with his fingers he hauled himself upwards. It was only the work of a minute to reach the summit of the wall, and to sling his legs over and face into the garden. He was in luck. The branches of the conker tree hid him from any prying cyos inside the house.

He leaned forward and gingerly grasped the end of one of the branches. Inching his way across he soon reached the relative safety of the trunk, and sliding down he grasped at the ripening conkers. Reaching the ground he began to gather up the ripest specimens from around the base of the tree and cram them into his pockets.

It was at that moment he realised he was being watched.

Trying to appear perfectly at ease and wishing that the bulges in his pockets were not quite so noticeable, Billy straightened up and turned around. About ten yards away stood an old lady. Her clothes were dark and unsuited to the weather. Her face was grey and almost merged with the white of her hair.
Billy cleared his throat.
'Er, excuse me missus, I'm sorry….er…. I just thought that, well that you might not want all these conkers for yourself…'
The old lady turned away and walked quickly towards the old timber outhouse built onto the side of the stone kitchen.

'Huh, deaf old bat!'

Billy wasted no time in scurrying back to the tree trunk and clambering his way upwards to the overhanging branch. A moment later he was dropping back into the lane outside.

At the tea table that evening Billy removed his new found treasure from his pockets.

'Billy Barnes, you're not going to bring all those into the house, all covered in cow muck, and expect me to put them in the oven for you?' declared his mother as she speared sausages in the frying pan.

'Where did you get them lad?' His father leaned over to examine them, 'They look real beauties!'

Billy scooped them into a neat pile on the kitchen table.

'From the Manor House.'

Billy's father put down his evening paper.

'Where?'

'The old Manor House. You know, at the bottom of the lane.'

Billy's mother dropped the fork into the frying pan.

'Now how did you get in there?'

'Easy!' Billy grinned proudly. Even his Dad hadn't managed to get inside when he was a lad. 'I climbed up over the wall. It's starting to crack. There were plenty of foot holds. The only thing was I nearly got caught!'

'Oh?' Billy's father was listening intently.

'Yes, I was just collecting them off the ground at the foot of the tree when I had the feeling I was being watched. I looked up and there was this old lady. Lucky for me she was deaf as a post and blind as a bat as well. She never said a word. Just disappeared into that old wooden part of the house.'

Billy's mother switched off the gas.

'Get your coat!'

'Eh? What for Mum? I thought we were just about to have tea?'

'Get your coat and get down to your Uncle John's this minute. Tell him what you just told us.'

'But Mum, my tea! I'm starving!'

'It'll be here when you get back. Now get down to your Uncle John's this minute and tell him, word for word.'

Billy, impressed by the urgency in his mother's voice, pulled on his coat. When he had gone out of the door his mother sighed and looked hard at her husband.

'Our John was right then,' she said, 'that story he told us when he was a lad?' Billy's father nodded.

Billy knocked on the front door of his Uncle John's house. His uncle was a few years older than Billy's mother. He too had lived in the village all his life.

'Come in! Come in!' Uncle John ushered Billy into the kitchen. 'What can I do for you?'

Billy shuffled uncomfortably.

'I don't really know Uncle. It's me Mum. She told me to come straight away. Told me to tell you what happened this afternoon.'

Uncle John pulled up a chair and nodded for Billy to continue.

'Well, this afternoon, while I was looking for conkers I thought I'd see if there was any way of getting into the Manor House garden…'

Billy eventually came to the end of his story.

'So I was lucky really. She was deaf as a post and blind too I reckon. She never noticed me. I was almost standing on top of her as well! But she walked past me without saying a word!'

Uncle John pulled out his pipe and began to rummage in the table drawer for a box of matches.

'Well, I'll tell *you* a story now,' he said.

His hand closed on a matchbox and he struck a match and applied it carefully to the bowl of his pipe.

'About four hundred years ago there was a big family living in the Manor House. Youngest was a boy, not much older than you are now. One day the family had been out, taking their pleasure, all apart from the youngest boy, who had been stricken by a fever. He had stayed in bed, with his old nanny to care for him. Seems even in those days the folk who lived there weren't too keen on village children helping themselves to those conkers. Nanny had strict orders not to allow anyone into the gardens. Anyway it seems she was just preparing a pan of broth for the boy when she heard a noise outside, near the horse chestnut tree.

She rushed outside to find some village lads cavorting about and stuffing their pockets with conkers. She shouted at them and then returned to the boy. She was too late. Whilst she'd been outside a stray ember from the fire had sparked onto the matting and straw in the kitchen and within minutes the whole place was alight. She ran back in to rescue the child. Neither of them came out.'

Uncle John puffed his pipe appreciatively.

'This old lady you saw,' he continued, 'would she have been wearing very dark clothes? Had white hair and a waxen face?'

Billy nodded, half in a daze.

'You say she disappeared into that wooden outhouse built onto the kitchen?'

Billy nodded again.

Uncle John got up from his chair and began to rummage in a cupboard on the other side of the kitchen.

'There's no wooden outhouse there now Billy.'

Uncle John appeared to find what he was looking for in the dark recesses of the cupboard.

'It burned down four hundred years ago. There are no wooden outbuildings there now at all.'

Billy sat silent as the truth dawned. Eventually he found his voice.

'But how do you know all this Uncle John?'

Uncle John's face creased into a gentle smile. He opened his hand and there, resting in his palm, was a hard, shiny conker.

'I was keen on conkers too when I was a lad. Look at this. It was a three hundreder. Unbroken record. You ask your Dad. And guess where I got it?'

Printed in Great Britain
by Amazon